Teddy's First Christmas

AMANDA DAVIDSON

COLLINS

For Andrew

William Collins Sons & Co Ltd
London · Glasgow · Sydney · Auckland
Toronto · Johannesburg

First published 1982
Second impression 1983

ISBN 0 00 195842 9
Origination by Culver Graphics Litho Ltd
Printed in Italy
by Sagdos for Imago Publishing Ltd

It is Christmas Eve. Everyone is asleep.

Look at the presents piled under the tree.

Look at the big red box with the ribbon on top.

There's somebody inside. . . .

It’s Teddy!

Hello Teddy.

"What's that?" says Teddy.

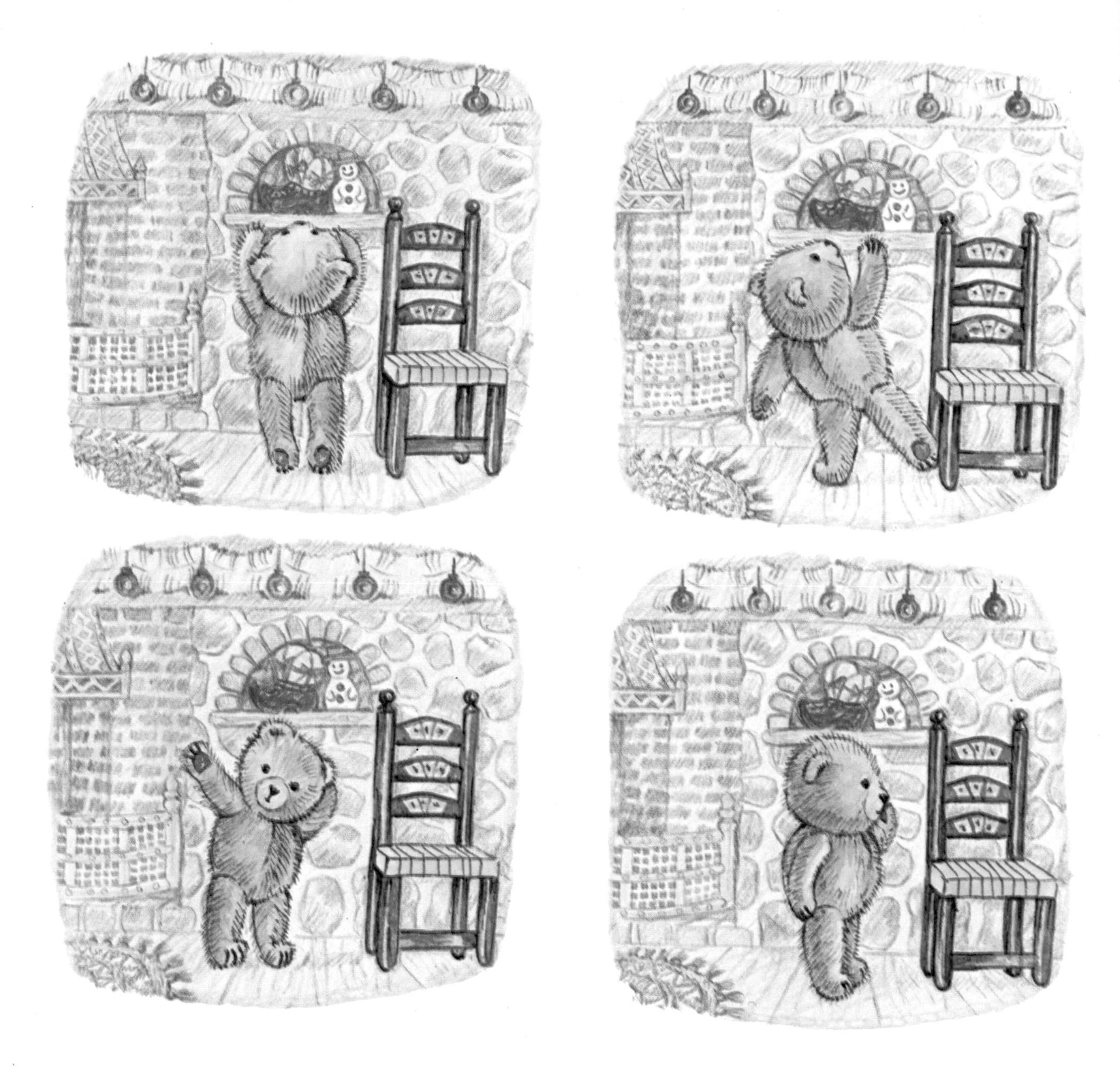

"It's very hard to reach."

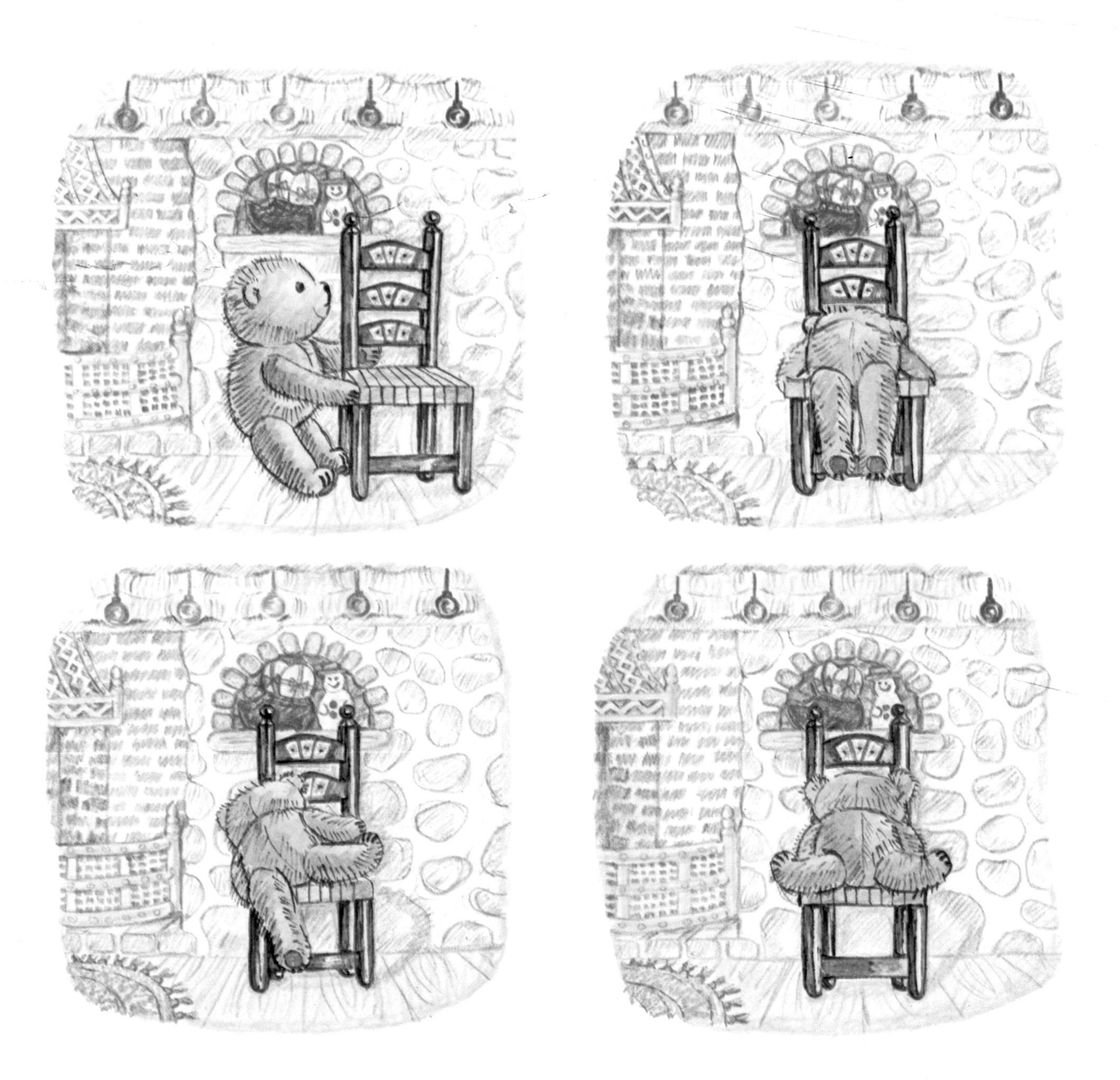

"What shall I do?"

Be **careful**, Teddy.

Oh dear! Up you get.

"Who's that?" says Teddy.

"I'd like to talk to her."

Be **careful**, Teddy.

Oh dear! Up you get.

"And what's this?" says Teddy.

“I’ll pull it and see.”

Pull, pull, and . . .

up in the air . . . and . . .

back in the box,

ready for Christmas morning!

HORRIBLE HAIRCARE

ANITA CROY

raintree
a Capstone company — publishers for children

Raintree is an imprint of Capstone Global Library Limited, a company incorporated in England and Wales having its registered office at 264 Banbury Road, Oxford, OX2 7DY – Registered company number: 6695582

www.raintree.co.uk
myorders@raintree.co.uk

Produced for Raintree by Calcium
Editors: Sarah Eason and Tim Cooke
Designers: Clare Webber and Lynne Lennon
Picture researcher: Rachel Blount
Originated by Capstone Global Library Ltd
Printed and bound in India

ISBN 978 1 4747 7765 0 (hardback)
ISBN 978 1 4747 7768 1 (paperback)

British Library Cataloguing in Publication Data
A full catalogue record for this book is available from the British Library.

Acknowledgements
We would like to thank the following for permission to reproduce photographs: Cover: Shutterstock: Dean Bertoncelj; Inside: Library of Congress: p. 32; Shutterstock: Everett Historical: pp. 4, 19b, 27t, 34; HiddenCatch: pp. 1, 42; Rosa Jay: p. 11t; JPC-PROD: p. 15b; Evgeny Kabardin: p. 41t; Kdonmuang: p. 41b; Merrymuuu: p. 43t; Photographee.eu: p. 40; Photolinc: p. 17t; Kristin Smith: p. 37; Victorian Traditions: p. 25b; Mahathir Mohd Yasin: p. 43b; Wikimedia Commons: pp. 13, 17b, 35b; Anagoria: p. 9b; Guillaume Blanchard: p. 8; Mathew Brady: p. 27b; Louis Calvete: p. 28, 31b; CeStu: p. 5t; Cornelis Jonson van Ceulen: p. 19t; Sir Anthony Van Dyck: p. 18; José Echenagusia Errazquin: p. 7b; Roger Fenton: p. 26; Unknown, probably Jean-Baptiste André Gautier-Dagoty: p. 21t; 1863: excavated by Léon Heuzey and Henri Daumet: p. 10; Jebulon: p. 7t; Nicolas de Largillière: p. 22; Nicolas de Larmessin: p. 20; Albert Lynch: p. 14; Maarjaara: p. 6; MGM: p. 30; After Pierre Mignard: p. 21b; Naval History & Heritage Command: p. 29t; Jac. de Nijs/Anefo; Restoration by User:Adam Cuerden: p. 33; Fred C. Palmer: p. 29b; Ashley Pomeroy: p. 35t; Purchased in 1811 from Rondanini Palace: p. 11b; Rauantiques: p. 24; Tim Schapker: p. 39; Joseph Karl Stieler: p. 25t; Titian: p. 16; U.S. National Archives and Records Administration: pp. 21t, 36; United Press International, photographer unknown: p. 38; Walters Art Museum: p. 9t; Wellcome Images: p. 23; Workshop of Rogier van der Weyden: p. 12; Wonderlane: p. 5b; Francisco de Zurbarán: p. 15t.

Every effort has been made to contact copyright holders of material reproduced in this book. Any omissions will be rectified in subsequent printings if notice is given to the publisher.

CONTENTS

Chapter 1

ANCIENT - HAIR -

Hair has always been associated with attractiveness and power. Over the centuries, different styles and colours have come in and out of fashion.

Around 1500 BC, the Assyrians ruled Babylonia in the Middle East. Their skill at dyeing, curling and layering their hair made them the leading hairstylists in the region.

GET CURLING!

For the Assyrians, hairstyles gave them status. It was not just hair that was styled in Babylon. Beards were also oiled, tinted and perfumed. As a sign of just how important they were, Assyrian women sometimes wore false beards during meetings. Fashionable Assyrian hair and beard styles included the **symmetrical cut**. People curled their hair and beards by wrapping it around iron bars that were heated in a fire. They sometimes had accidents and set their hair alight!

Assyrian men curled their hair and beards into elaborate designs.

THAT'S MY COLOUR

Before they were conquered by the Assyrians, Babylonian men liked to show their power by dusting their long, flowing locks with gold dust. The emperors of Persia, in what is now Iran, laced their beards with gold thread. Gold made them feel more powerful. The ancient Egyptians loved coloured hair. The wigs and **hair extensions** they often wore were blue, green, blonde and gold.

This stone carving shows the head of a Celtic warrior. These warriors dyed their hair blue and went into battle naked to terrify their enemies.

It was the ancient Greeks who first decided that blondes had more fun. In the Greek world, the lighter the hair, the better. The Romans who conquered Greece in the second century BC copied Greek styles. They lightened their hair using wood ash and various **minerals**. When darker colours were "in", copper filings, oak apples and a mixture of blood-sucking **leeches** soaked in wine and vinegar did the job – as long as the gunk did not slide straight off your head!

The long-haired, long-bearded Merovingians, who lived in what is now France between the sixth and eighth centuries AD, believed their strength came from their red hair. The Celts put chalk or lime in their hair to sleek it back or spike it. They thought it would frighten their enemies.

For Greek women, light hair echoed the hair of the gods.

THE POWER
- OF HAIR -

More than any other part of the body, hair has a special status. Some of the best-known myths and legends over the centuries have given hair a starring role.

The popular fairy tale of Rapunzel is based on an Iranian myth that is more than 3,000 years old. In the story, Rapunzel is imprisoned in a tower. She grows her hair so long that she can lower it to allow a prince to climb up and release her. They fall in love and are married.

The Greek god Apollo was often potrayed wearing a crown around his head.

LEAVE MY HAIR ALONE

Rapunzel's story reflects the power often associated with hair. Native American warriors scalped their victims, cutting the skin and hair from their heads. The Manchu rulers of China forced their subjects to shave off all but a single long piece of hair as a sign of submission. Meanwhile, slaves everywhere often had their hair shaved off to show their low status in society.

IT'S ALL GREEK TO ME

In one Greek myth, the priestess Medusa was famous for her beauty and her gorgeous cascading hair. The goddess

Athena was so jealous that she turned Medusa's flowing locks into a head of writhing snakes. Anyone who looked at Medusa was turned to stone.

The Roman emperor Julius Caesar covered his balding head with a crown made from laurel leaves. He was copying the Greeks, who awarded laurel crowns to athletes for winning events in the Olympic Games. Thanks to Caesar, the laurel crown became a symbol of **nobility** in Rome. It was worn by wealthy Romans even if they had hair.

Medusa was finally killed by the Greek hero Perseus, son of the god Zeus.

hello beautiful

In the Bible, Samson was an Israelite warrior with long, flowing hair that gave him great strength. He fell in love with Delilah. She was paid by Samson's enemies to discover the secret of his strength. She kept asking him until eventually, he told her. One night, she chopped off his hair while he slept. When he woke up, all of his strength was gone.

When Delilah cut Samson's hair, he lost all of his formidable strength.

FALSE - HAIR -

The ancient Egyptians knew a thing or two about hair. They believed hair was sacred, so they cut off their own hair and wore wigs instead!

In Egypt's hot climate, most people shaved their heads or kept their hair short to reduce sweating. They did not wash their hair often, because they believed it would disturb the spirit who looked after the head. A wig was cooler to wear and easier to keep clean.

IT'S HOT IN HAIR!

The richest Egyptians wore wigs made from real hair. Most people wore wigs of wool, palm fibres or straw to protect their heads from the sun. Some people put a cake of perfumed wax on top of the wig. The wax melted and kept the wearer cool. Egyptians used wet mud or a jelly made from **quince** soaked in water to set their hair.

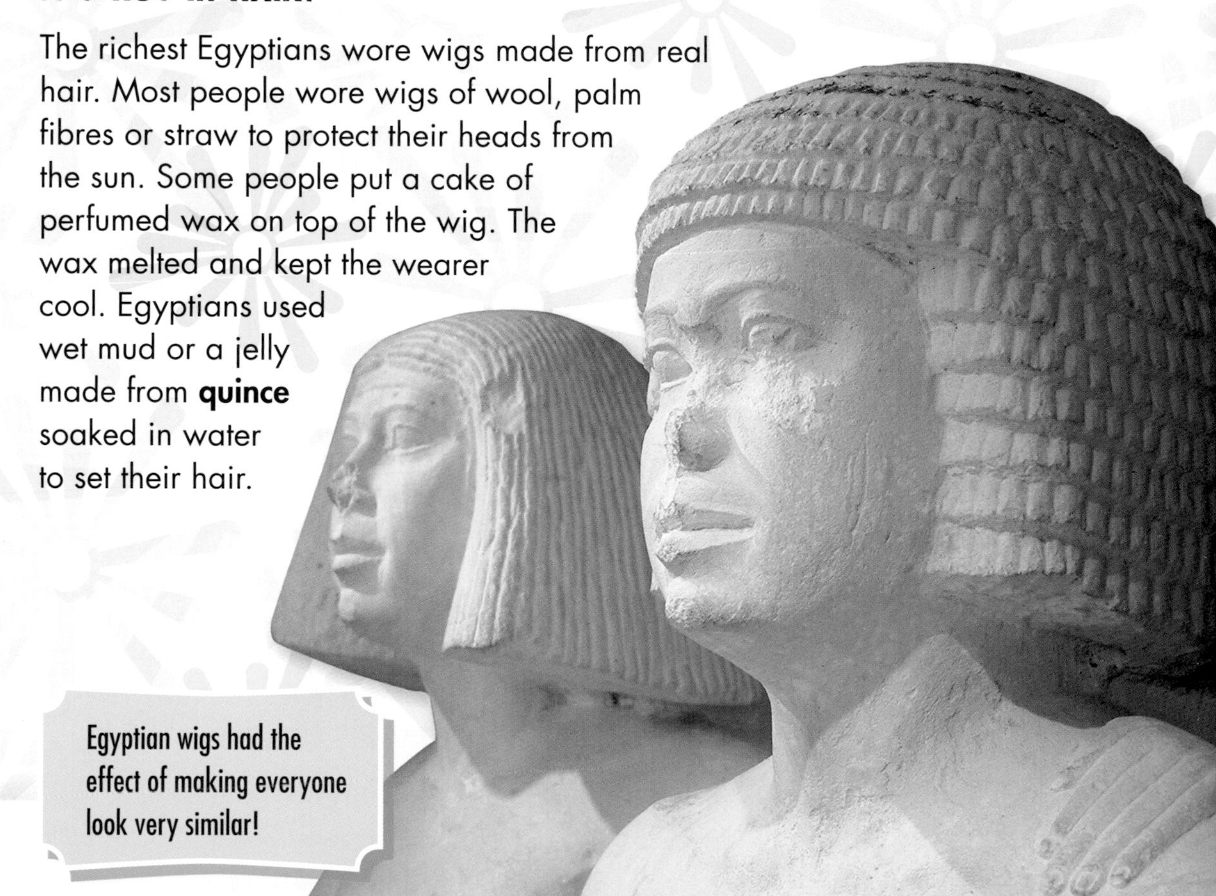

Egyptian wigs had the effect of making everyone look very similar!

CHANGING STYLES

Egyptian wigs started out small and curled, but over centuries they became more elaborate. Some large wigs had long sides that fell down to the wearer's chest. Later wigs went for maximum bling, with lots of plaits woven around gold tubes and sprinkled with real gold powders. For men, the look was often completed with a fake beard – and even some powerful women wore fake beards. To demonstrate their power, **pharaohs** liked their fake beards to be made from solid gold.

An Egyptian woman with hair down over her shoulders plays an instrument called a sistrum.

hello beautiful

Queen Hatshepsut ruled Egypt in the fifteenth century BC. She was only the second female pharaoh. As a sign of her power, all official statues of the queen showed her with a fake gold beard, just like the male pharaohs. The beard may have helped her image. Hatshepsut was one of the most successful of all the pharaohs, ruling for 20 years.

Hatshepsut expanded Egyptian trade and commissioned many new buildings.

THE CLASSICAL - WORLD -

The ancient Greeks favoured the natural look when it came to their hair. The Romans, as usual, mixed and matched trends from both Egypt and Greece.

Before the fifth century BC, Greek women put fresh flowers in their hair and wore it long. Later, they began pulling their hair back into a knot or coil at the back, called a chignon.

Two Greek women pick flowers with their hair tied up behind their heads in hair nets.

AU NATUREL

The most fashionable hair was blonde, following a trend set by the Greek goddesses, who were depicted with light hair. Women who could afford it achieved a yellow hue by sprinkling gold or **saffron** powder in their hair. Women who were poorer lightened their hair with a mixture of **potash** water and yellow flowers. The Romans copied some Greek fashions, but overall they preferred the complex hair designs they knew from Queen Cleopatra and other prominent Egyptians. Romans who did not have slaves to style their hair, had this done at a hair salon.

KEEP YOUR HAIR ON

Baldness was not a good look in Greece and Rome. In ancient Greece, a popular potion to restore the hair included rose essence, wine and olive oil. Another was a blend of cumin, pigeon droppings, crushed horseradish and nettles. Failing that, men simply smeared their heads with pigeon droppings or goat's urine. The Romans had all sorts of baldness remedies. When the emperor Julius Caesar's hair started to fall out, he applied a paste of bear grease, deer marrow, horses' teeth and ground-up mice. When that failed, he gave up and started wearing his laurel crown.

The Greek philosopher Aristotle tried goat's urine as a cure for baldness.

to die for

Hair fashions changed quickly in ancient Rome – even for statues. When Roman women had their portraits sculpted, they got the sculptor to create removable hair. That allowed them easily to replace old styles with the latest fashion. Hairstyles changed so often that historians use the hair in statues and paintings as a handy way to identify periods in Roman history.

Even Roman statues had the lastest hairstyles – no matter how unflattering!

Chapter 2

THE MIDDLE - AGES -

During the Middle Ages, hair revealed a lot about a person, including their position in society, whether they were married and even their religious beliefs.

Hair was a low priority for medieval women. For much of the Middle Ages, the idea of beauty was based on having as high a forehead as possible. Women achieved the effect by plucking their eyebrows and pushing back their hair so it could barely be seen.

COVER UP

In the early Middle Ages, wealthy women wore their hair loose or in two long plaits on either side of the head. Married women wore their hair tied back in a chignon covered with fabric or a woven net. Some women plaited their hair and coiled it above their ears.

As the Middle Ages went on, there was a new focus on **modesty**. Christianity, Islam and Judaism all condemned long hair as encouraging **immoral** behaviour.

This portrait shows Isabella of Portugal in around 1450 with her hair pushed back.

Women achieved both a modest appearance and a high forehead by concealing their hair with a hat, hood or **veil**. One popular medieval style was a very tall conical hat with a veil at the front.

This artwork shows Russian priests with beards and long hair. Later, Christian priests turned against this fashion.

WHAT ABOUT MEN?

Until the fifteenth century, the Catholic Church set the rules on personal grooming, including how long men's hair should be, whether or not men grew beards, and acceptable hair coverings for women. The Church said that hair should be short, so servants and the poor all wore their hair short. Although more important men often had slightly longer hair, even monarchs had to obey the rules. In the ninth century, the French king Louis II followed Church teaching and had his long hair cut as short as a monk's. In 1073, Pope Gregory banned beards among the clergy, and soon everyone stopped growing beards. In 1096, the Archbishop of Rouen in France announced that any man with a beard would be expelled from the Church! Even in the twelfth century, King Henry I of England was forced to cut his hair and shave off his beard after a priest delivered a strong sermon against long hair and beards.

DO IT - YOURSELF -

Medieval barbers often doubled as doctors. They removed patients' blood and set bones, as well as shaving beards. They did not have time to cut hair too!

Joan of Arc became a national heroine when she led French soldiers into battle against an English army.

Most people cut their own hair. It was quite easy to keep up with trends, because they moved slowly. The bowl-shaped pageboy cut for men lasted from the eleventh to the sixteenth century. It might have been so popular because it was so easy to do: people simply placed a bowl over the head and cut off any exposed hair.

EARLY TRENDS

One of the first women to have a pageboy haircut was the fifteenth-century French soldier Joan of Arc. It only became a trend for women around 500 years later, in the early twentieth century. Monks' hairstyles changed even more slowly. From the eighth century, a monk's hair was shaved off except for a circular strip around the head. This style was called a tonsure, and showed that monks renounced worldly fashions.

HAIR TREATMENTS

Women's hair might have been hidden under hats and veils, but they still wanted it to look good. There were all sorts of home recipes for hair products, including a potion made by boiling a lizard in olive oil. Egg whites gave the hair body and structure, while nettles mixed in vinegar cured dry scalps. A mixture of vinegar, berry juice, broom and sage got rid of insects called lice. Bear fat was said to increase hair growth and lanolin was a popular conditioner. It was made from the oil trapped in sheep's wool together with flax seeds and hemp oil.

A monk's tonsure was a sign that he was more interested in spiritual things than in looking good.

to die for

Hair dyeing was in – and it took a while! For blonde hair, people boiled walnut shells and bark, added flowers, and put the liquid on their hair. They covered the hair with leaves and left it for two days. Then they added henna, saffron and other ingredients and left it all for another three days. After all that, at least the colour was said to last!

Walnut shells are still used as a source of dye today.

Chapter 3

THE EARLY - MODERN WORLD -

As Europe left the Dark Ages behind, hairstyles became more showy. In the sixteenth century, an English queen changed how people wore their hair.

In this painting of Mary and Jesus, the artist Titian painted Mary with red hair, which was fashionable in Venice, where he lived.

At the end of the Middle Ages, women still wore their hair under caps to please the Catholic Church. These caps were anything but modest, however. Made from fabrics such as velvet and covered with jewels and ribbons, the most glamorous caps came from Milan in Italy. They were only worn by the most fashionable women.

HIDING AWAY

Although the church disapproved, the fashion for coloured hair was so popular that some women reached for their home-made dyes. A popular dye for blonde hair used henna, gorse flowers, saffron, eggs and calf kidneys. In sixteenth-century Venice, women achieved a fashionable copper red colour by putting **caustic soda** on their hair and then sitting in bright sunlight.

Eggs were a standard ingredient in recipes for creating yellow hair.

Women who wanted their hair to be jet black achieved the effect by using combs made of lead. However, the poisonous lead caused some women to suffer kidney failure.

RED-HAIRED QUEEN

Queen Elizabeth I ruled from 1558 to 1603, and during that time she set the hair fashions of the day. Elizabeth's red hair meant that red hair became a must for English nobles. Men dyed their hair and beards red to show their loyalty to the queen. Women dyed their hair, too, but they used a dye that contained sulphur and lead, which are both **toxic**. The poisons caused sickness, headaches and nosebleeds.

When Elizabeth's hair thinned, she began wearing wigs. She owned more than 80 wigs in a range of styles, all made from expensive imported hair. No one else could afford so many wigs – but at least wearing wigs did not make them ill.

In 1587, Elizabeth had her cousin, Mary Queen of Scots, beheaded for trying to seize the throne. As Mary's head fell to the ground, her **auburn**-haired wig also fell off, revealing her real hair, which was short and grey.

When she became an older woman, Queen Elizabeth I usually wore a wig with short, curled red hair.

WAR OF THE
- HAIRSTYLES -

Who would have thought that two contrasting hairstyles could get caught up in a war? That is just what happened during the English Civil War in the seventeenth century.

Charles I became king of England in 1625. He and his followers, known as Cavaliers, had long, curly hair or wigs topped with elaborate hats or ostrich feathers. Their clothes were also ornate, with ribbons, lace and jewels.

THE KINGS

For many people in England, the appearance of these Cavaliers showed that they were **vain** and interested only in pleasure. Their political opponents, known as Puritans, were led by Oliver Cromwell. They looked

This triple portrait shows King Charles I in 1636, giving a clear view of the long, curled hair that his opponents disliked so much.

very different. Puritans cut their hair short and refused to wear wigs as a sign of their loyalty to the Protestant branch of Christianity. They wore plain, dark clothes, in contrast to the flamboyant clothes worn at court.

CIVIL WAR

The appearances of the two groups reflected very different ideas about politics. In 1642, these differences led to civil war. Charles and the Royalists lost the war. In 1649, Charles was put on trial for treason, found guilty and then beheaded. Just before he died, it is believed he asked the executioner, "Is my hair well?" After Charles' death, the Puritans governed England. Life was not much fun: there was lots of hard work and prayer – and no glamorous hair!

The Puritans believed in a sense of duty and hard work, and rejected excessive luxury and pleasure.

to die for

The Puritans had strong views on how hair should be worn. For men it had to be short, off the face and definitely uncurled. The Cavaliers called the Puritans "Roundheads" because of the shape of their hair (remember the pudding-bowl look?). Women could have long hair – but it had to be hidden underneath a plain white cap.

A Puritan family with plain clothes and simple hairstyles share a meal in a home without any decoration.

BIG
- HAIR -

France's Sun King, Louis XIV, began an era of excess in fashion, with towering wigs and extravagant decoration.

The fashions in France could hardly have been more different from the modest Puritan styles of England. At Louis' court at Versailles, "more" was always better. During his long reign from 1643 to 1715, Louis increasingly wore wigs. Not only did they make him look taller – they also hid his bald head. Louis' male courtiers followed, wearing wigs with curls cascading below the shoulders and a fringe across the forehead.

Madame de Fontanges is said to have created a hairdressing sensation – by accident.

FRANCE RULES

In contrast, women's hair seemed quite restrained. The fashionable look was to pin the hair up, leaving just one tumbling lock free. Then Madame de Fontanges, one of the king's favourite companions, set a new fashion when she lost her hat while out hunting. She piled her hair into a loose knot on top of her head and secured it with a lace-edged garter. Louis approved and the "fontange" was born. It stayed in fashion for the next three centuries.

PILE IT HIGH

By the late eighteenth century, women wore their hair in piles up to 90 centimetres (3 feet) tall. The hair was supported by horsehair pads and stiffened with a paste of flour and water. Courtiers competed to decorate their hair. One woman had a model of her son's nursery in her hair, while another had a ship in full sail. This tall hair gave its wearers headaches, sore necks and little sleep. In addition, it took so long to create the styles that they were only redone once a month. The unwashed, floured hair became infested with **vermin**. Women cut slits in the stiffened walls of hair to allow head lice to escape.

Women added extensions to their natural hair.

Louis XIV set hair trends across Europe. When his hair started to thin, he employed 48 wig-makers to keep him supplied with wigs to hide his early baldness. Once the king started wearing a wig, even courtiers with plenty of hair followed. The fashion for wigs took off not only at Versailles but also across Europe.

Once Louis XIV took to wearing wigs, everyone followed suit.

WORLD OF - THE WIG -

It would take a revolution to stop the French wearing their wigs. But they continued to be popular in England until the next century.

In France, expensive wigs were a status symbol for most of the eighteenth century. Then, in 1789, the French overthrew their king and the nobility in a revolution. Overnight, wearing fancy wigs went out of fashion.

BIG WIGS

In Britain, by contrast, wigs remained a sign of social status. Anyone who could afford a wig wore one. People who could not afford to buy a wig styled their hair so it looked like a wig! In colonial America, meanwhile, wigs were associated with the colonies' British rulers. On the eve of the American Revolution (1765–1783), Benjamin Franklin opposed the wearing of wigs as a sign of opposition to British rule in America.

The best wigs were so expensive that people left them to their families in their wills.

A PUFF OF POWDER

In the late eighteenth century, it became fashionable to powder wigs with **starch**. The powder was thrown into the air so it settled on the wig. Wealthy people had a special room just for powdering wigs, or wore special dressing gowns and put a paper cone over their faces to avoid getting covered in the powder. Women preferred pastel shades of powder, such as pink and violet, while men went for white or grey. Poor people dusted their wigs with flour. Getting caught in the rain ruined a powdered wig. Wigs also had a habit of bursting into flames if a wearer sat too close to the fire.

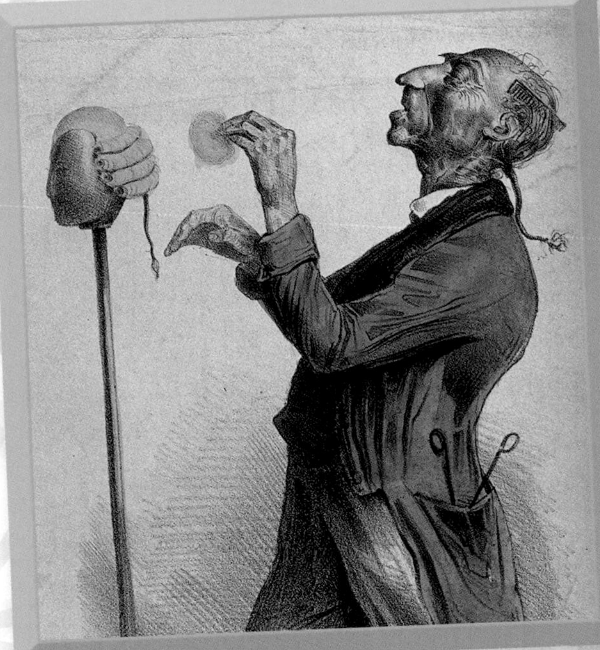

A barber powders a wig supported on a special wig stand.

to die for

In 1798, British Prime Minister William Pitt introduced a tax on wig powder. One estimate is that people at the time were using enough flour and starch on their wigs to make bread for 50,000 people, so Pitt saw a chance to raise money. However, his tax was so unpopular that people stopped using powder on their wigs – and soon stopped wearing wigs, too.

Chapter 4

THE NINETEENTH - CENTURY -

As the nineteenth century dawned, the impact of the French Revolution was still being felt. Natural hair was back in fashion and wigs were a thing of the past.

Early in the century, the Empress Josephine, wife of the French emperor Napoleon, set the fashions. Women copied Josephine's hairdo, which was inspired by ancient Greece. The hair was curled at the front and gathered into a chignon at the back, with minimal ornament.

Empress Josephine started what was called the Empire look, based on ancient Greek styles.

MALE MODELS

For men, the model was the English **dandy** Beau Brummell. Brummell was said to employ three hairdressers – one to cut the back of his hair, one to cut the right side and one to cut the left – all at the same time. With his long, curled hair, he looked like a **Romantic** poet. The Romantic artistic movement praised long hair as being natural and wild. The days of the wig were gone.

VICTORIAN ERA

In 1837, Victoria was crowned queen of Great Britain. For the next 60 years she dictated hair fashion in Britain and Europe. The queen favoured a modest appearance. Her hair was natural, but she concealed it under a **bonnet** or a cap. Ladies were considered undressed if they left home without a bonnet. Women never cut their hair. Although young girls were allowed to wear their hair long, married women had to put their hair up and keep it hidden.

In Victorian England, a modest appearance was a sign of good behaviour. The Victorians believed that a woman's hair revealed her personality: curly-haired women were thought to be sweeter and kinder than women with straight hair. Women who dared to show off their long hair were considered shocking. Such daring women were often associated with **bohemian** artistic movements or were actresses in the theatre.

The Romantic composer Ludwig van Beethoven had wild, flowing hair.

Even late in the nineteenth century, women kept their hair hidden beneath bonnets.

WATCH THOSE - WHISKERS! -

In the middle of the nineteenth century, men went beard and moustache crazy. Following the lead of military heroes of the day, clean-shaven faces were out of fashion.

The military were to thank for the nineteenth century craze for facial hair. With the exception of Bavarian soldiers, who were banned from growing facial hair, soldiers across Europe sported moustaches and beards.

KEEPING WARM

The elegant whiskers of earlier centuries were replaced by huge, bushy beards and long whiskers that left just enough room to reveal the mouth. The Crimean War (1854–1856), when British soldiers fought Russians in the Crimea, was the inspiration for this bushy look. The freezing winter temperatures and a lack of shaving soap led the British army to lift its ban on beards. Full facial hair was one way of keeping warm – and it was free!

British soldiers grew facial hair in the Crimean War as a defence against the bitterly cold winters.

OUR AMERICAN COUSIN

In the United States, it did not take much for men to abandon shaving, which was still tricky and unsafe. The market was flooded with equipment, including a portable heated curler to curl the moustache ends. The moustache cup had a raised lip-guard to keep drinks from touching the hair. In 1861, the character Lord Dundreary in a popular play sported magnificent side-whiskers. These whiskers, known as "dundrearies", became popular in both Britain and the United States. (By coincidence, Abraham Lincoln, the first US president with a beard, was watching the same play – *Our American Cousin* – when he was assassinated in 1865.)

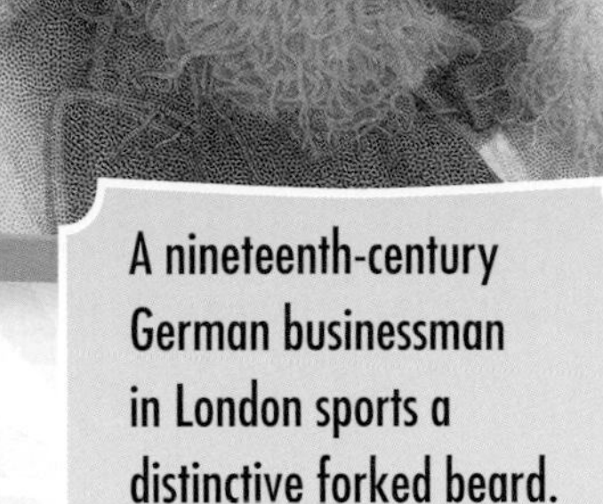

A nineteenth-century German businessman in London sports a distinctive forked beard.

During the American Civil War (1861–1865), Union Major General Ambrose Burnside (right) sported a distinctive moustache and whiskers with a clean-shaven chin. He created a new fashion for unbroken bushy facial hair, named "burnsides" after him. The two parts of the name were later reversed to give the style the name "sideburns", which is still used today.

GIVE US
- A WAVE -

When the curling tong appeared near the end of the nineteenth century, it was not as modern as it seemed. In fact, it was more than 5,000 years old!

In 1872, Marcel Grateau opened a hairdressing salon in Paris, France. As a teenager, Grateau had worked grooming horses. He put that training to good use!

CURL, BABY, CURL

The ancient Babylonians had learned to curl the hair by wrapping it around hot iron rods. Grateau used a heated curling iron to make tight, frizzy waves that sat close to his clients' heads. In a rush one day, he used the curling iron upside down – and created a new craze. This "Marcel Wave" looked more natural than the earlier tight curls. It also worked equally well on curly and straight hair. Grateau patented his curling tong in 1890, and the style spread. The Marcel Wave would stay in fashion for the next 50 years.

In the early twentieth century, waved hairstyles became more elaborate.

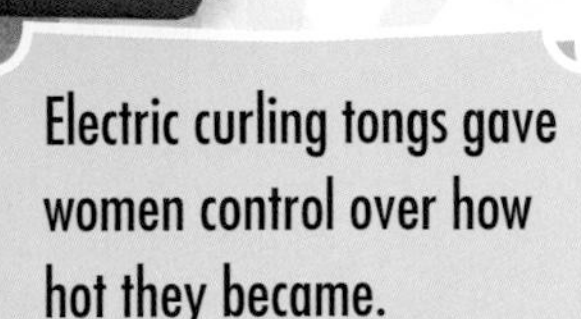

Electric curling tongs gave women control over how hot they became.

to die for

Curling tongs had been making waves since the Babylonians, but before Grateau invented electric tongs, they could be dangerous. The tongs were heated in fires, so there was no way to regulate how hot they got. Women paid the price of scalp burns and singed hair to get their hair curled just right.

CROWNING GLORY

Even before Grateau's innovation, hair had become big business. Nineteenth-century magazines devoted many words to instructing women just how to get the right "look". They advised washing the hair once a month and gave precise details of how to dry and style the hair using curling tongs. It was a slow process because women had a lot of hair. To make the wave last longer, women rubbed **macassar oil** into their hair. The palm-based oil had become popular with men earlier in the century to give their hair a slicked-back look. The oil was so greasy that Victorian chairs had special macassar covers to stop the oil seeping into the cloth.

Victorian men achieved this typical slicked-back appearance by using macassar oil.

Chapter 5

THE TWENTIETH - CENTURY -

In the twentieth century, hairstyles came in and went out of fashion with dizzying speed. Meanwhile, the choice of hair products had never been greater.

In the first half of the century, film stars became trendsetters for all types of fashion, including hairstyles. Women watched their idols on the big screen and wanted to copy their look.

Veronica Lake wore her thick, long hair to one side.

I'M A STAR

In 1931, the film star Jean Harlow bleached her hair **platinum** using shop-bought dye. She made hair dyeing acceptable overnight. During World War II (1939–1945), authorities asked the actress Veronica Lake to change her hairstyle. Female factory workers who copied her long hair kept getting their hair caught in machinery! Hair in the 1950s was styled and **bouffant**, but in the late 1960s it became longer and more natural. In the 1970s, millions of women copied Farrah Fawcett's flicked

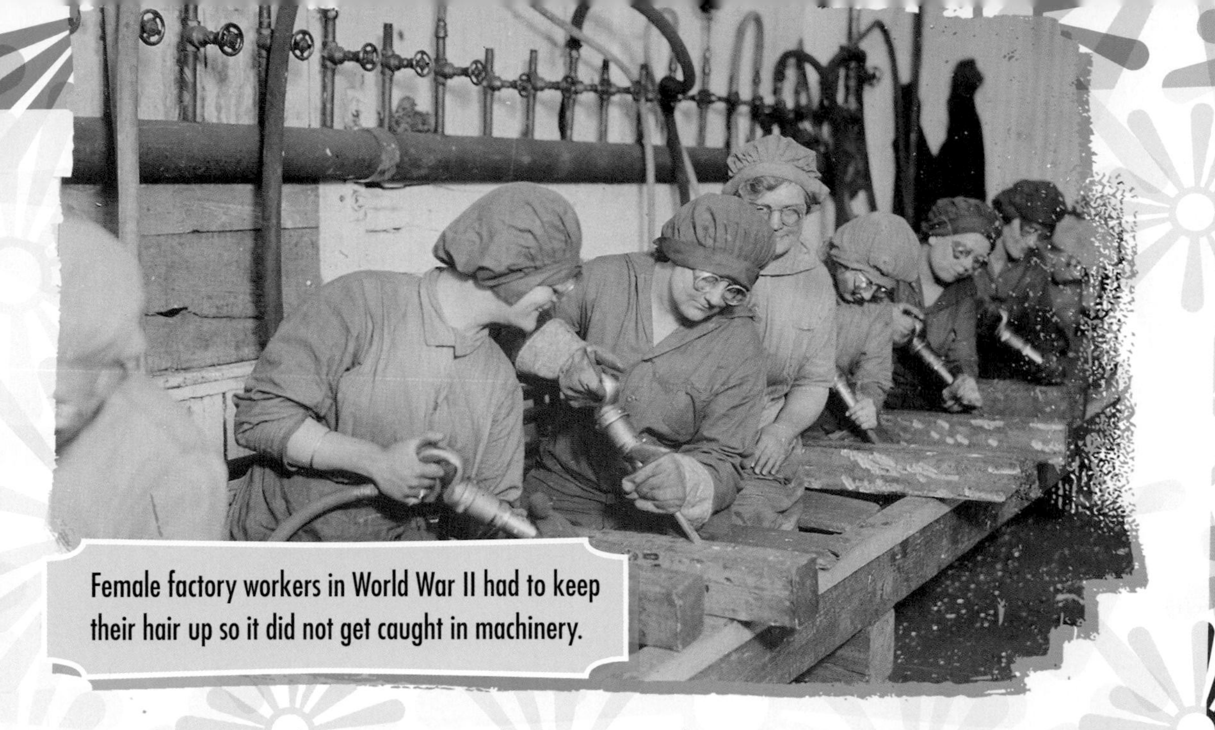

Female factory workers in World War II had to keep their hair up so it did not get caught in machinery.

blonde hair in the TV series *Charlie's Angels*. Two decades later, everyone wanted Jennifer Aniston's haircut in the hit comedy *Friends*. It wasn't only actresses who set trends. In the1990s, Princess Diana set many different hairstyle trends.

A MAN'S WORLD

Men's hair also went through decades of change thanks to the film and music industries. Men started the century slicking back their hair and sporting handlebar moustaches. In the 1930s, film star Clark Gable's pencil moustache was the look to copy. When Elvis Presley burst onto the music scene in the 1950s, men copied his combed-back hair and bushy sideburns. The mop tops of the Beatles set the trend in the 1960s and in the 1970s it was the long-haired, bearded hippies. In the 1990s, the **grunge** movement saw young men with long, matted hair like the singer Kurt Cobain.

This machine was built in 1923 to style the hair in a "permanent wave" (perm).

AFRICAN AMERICAN
- HAIR -

Early in the twentieth century, two African American businesswomen revolutionized haircare for black women in the United States.

African American women's hair looked and grew differently from Caucasian women's hair. For centuries, however, it had been treated the same. Most black Americans lacked the money to pay for their own haircare products.

In the early twentieth century, most black women tried to straighten their hair in order to style it.

BIG BUSINESS

Two women from slave families changed things for millions of other African American women. Annie Turnbo Malone set up a business selling hair straighteners and oils for black women in Illinois. In 1902, she moved her business to St. Louis. One of Malone's sales agents was Sarah Breedlove Davis. In 1905, a recipe for hair oil came to her in a dream. It became the basis of her own haircare business, under the name Madam C.J. Walker. Walker became one of the first self-made women millionaires in America. She sold shampoos and conditioning products just for African Americans, and employed black women in her factories.

Malone and Walker created a new market of speciality hair products. They invented hair irons and oils to straighten naturally curly African hair.

NOT SO STRAIGHT

Later in the century, some African American women rejected the idea of straightening their hair to make it resemble white women's hair. They saw this as a denial of their heritage. In the 1960s, some of them started to leave their hair in its natural "**Afro**" state as part of the **Black Pride** movement. They were making a political statement that they were proud of their African American heritage and would no longer accept white standards of beauty.

The "Afro" became a political statement for black women and men in the 1960s and 1970s.

to die for

For the first half of the twentieth century, beauty was segregated in the United States. African American women could not buy hair products from the same shops as white women. Madam C.J. Walker got around this by selling her products door-to-door in black neighbourhoods. Her best-selling products included coconut-oil shampoo and Glossine, a pressing oil to straighten and smooth the hair.

SHORT IS
- BEAUTIFUL -

Life changed dramatically after World War I ended in 1918. Short hair came into style for both men and women as the modern age really began.

During World War I (1914–1918), the US Navy introduced compulsory haircuts for all sailors. Before long, all the other branches of the military had followed suit.

OFF WITH YOUR HAIR

The rules were very strict: the hair on the top of the head could be no more than 2.5 centimetres (1 inch) long. That was short! After the war, the rules were relaxed to allow a whole 5 cm (2 inches). US forces were popular heroes after their victory in the war, so when they returned to the United States, other men copied their short haircuts. New styling products for men, such as Brylcreem, let men slick back their cropped hair to copy the stars of silent films.

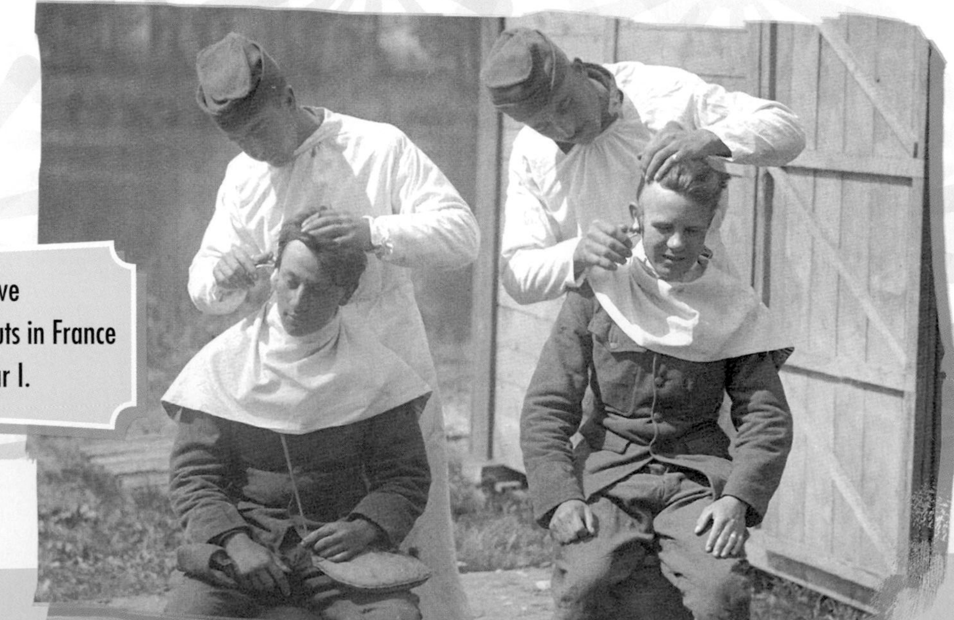

US soldiers receive regulation haircuts in France during World War I.

IN A FLAP

Queen Victoria died in 1901. Her death marked the beginning of the end for long hair hidden away under bonnets. World War I brought more change, as many women worked and earned their own money for the first time. Their new freedom brought new attitudes. Daring young women chopped their hair short into the fashionable "**bob**" cut worn by film stars known as the "It Girls". The number of hair salons increased in order to keep up with demand for the new short look, cut straight around the head. Curls were optional. The young women who led the way, known as **Flappers**, wore make-up and fashionable straight – and short – dresses.

Brylcreem, introduced in 1928, is a mixture of water, oil and beeswax.

Clara Bow became the original "It Girl" when she starred in the 1927 film *It*. She was the most famous star of silent films to survive the introduction of the "talkies". With her short, curly, bobbed dark hair, Bow helped set the trend for the daring, independent young women known as the Flappers.

Clara Bow's distinctive hair made her a screen idol in the late 1920s.

PILES OF - HAIR -

The 1950s saw a return to big hair thanks to new products that made hair easier to style. Soon women everywhere were sporting the look.

In the 1950s a new product found its way into the homes of millions of women. The spray can had been developed during World War II. It was mainly used for insect repellant. Now cosmetic companies used it to package a sticky, resin-based spray that kept hair from blowing around.

Jackie Kennedy was a fashion icon both during her time in the White House and afterwards.

ALL PUFFED UP

Hairspray allowed hairstylists and women at home to create all sorts of new looks. One popular early look was the bouffant. It was made famous in the early 1960s by the glamorous First Lady Jackie Kennedy, wife of US President John F. Kennedy. The bouffant was a puffed-out pageboy style created by winding hair in large rollers, allowing it to dry and then drowning it in hairspray. The bouffant led the way for many other types of puffed-up hair.

BUSY AS A BEE

Hairspray allowed women to backcomb their hair and then tease it into high mounds. The new styles were heaven for any woman who worried about having thin hair. Anyone who could not get the look with their own hair wore a hairpiece or a bouffant wig. The tallest style was the beehive, which appeared around 1958 and remained a hit into the 1960s. It needed a lot of hairspray to get enough height. It was sometimes called a B-52 after a large bomber, because its shape resembled the nose of the aircraft!

The beehive got its name from its resemblance to the conical shape of old-fashioned beehives.

Some of the biggest music stars of the 1960s wore beehives, including the soul singer Aretha Franklin and girl band the Ronettes. Some performers still wear beehives sometimes, including the singers Beyoncé and Adele. Today, possibly the most famous beehive belongs to Marge Simpson from the TV series *The Simpsons*. Once thought old-fashioned, the beehive is back with a bang!

HAIR
- TRIBES -

In the second half of the twentieth century, hair became tribal. Short, long or shaved hair were signs of people's ideas and loyalties.

The movement started in the mid-1960s, when the pop group The Beatles caused a scandal by growing their hair over their collars. Their fans called them the Mop Tops, and copied the haircut around the world.

HIPPIES AND AFROS

The hippie movement emerged in San Francisco a few years later. Hippies wanted to let their hair down – literally! Both men and women grew their hair long and never styled it, apart from putting flowers in it or wrapping **bandanas** around their heads. Meanwhile, African Americans also let their hair grow naturally as the Afro became popular. The performers Jimi Hendrix and James Brown both sported long Afros.

Pupils were sent home from some schools when they had haircuts like the Beatles.

THE SEVENTIES AND ON

The punk movement that started in Britain and the United States in the late 1970s introduced some of the most shocking hairstyles in history. Punks dyed their hair purple, green, blue – any colour that did not look natural – or shaved their heads, sometimes leaving a central strip of long hair that was gelled into an upright spike, called a mohican. In contrast, skinheads cropped their hair to look aggressive. With a reputation for violence, skinheads were best avoided.

The punk mohican was said to be inspired by the haircuts of Native American Mohicans in the nineteenth century.

In the late 1960s and early 1970s, the African American actress Marsha Hunt was as famous for her flamboyant Afro hairstyle as for her acting skills. Although she only had two lines to speak in the rock musical *Hair*, which played to full houses every night in London in 1968, Hunt grabbed the press headlines because of her striking look.

Chapter 6

THE TWENTY-FIRST CENTURY

Today, hair has never been freer for some people or more restricted for others. Religion and culture still play an important part in how we wear our hair.

Today, hair fashions come and go. Hair can be long or short, styled or unstyled, dyed or natural. Film stars, TV celebrities and even princesses still have an influence on the trends – but there is one significant difference in how we learn about new hairstyles.

A young woman records a hairstyling vlog as she shapes her hair with curling tongs.

ANYTHING GOES

Thanks to blogs and vlogs, the internet has become the go-to hair sourcebook of choice for millions of young people. Videos on creating a whole range of styles are widely available, as are reviews of haircare products. It has never been so easy to buy natural or organic hair products. Some hair dyes still use chemicals – although not the poisonous leads and sulphates of the past – but plant-based dyes like those our ancestors made are back in fashion. They include chamomile flowers to enhance blonde hair or henna to dye hair red.

RESTRICTIONS APPLY

Early in the twenty-first century, some religions still require women to keep their hair covered. Many branches of the Islamic faith require women to cover their hair, even though the rule is not explicitly stated in the Islamic holy book, the Qur'an. Muslim women wear coverings ranging from simple headscarves to hijabs that cover the head and burkas that cover their heads and faces. In some extreme Islamic cultures, not covering your hair is punishable by death. Some **orthodox** Jewish groups still expect married women to shave their heads on marriage and then wear a wig.

In the Christian world, many women wear a veil on their wedding day. Women who visit the Vatican in Rome to meet the Pope traditionally had to cover their heads with a black veil. Pope Francis, who became head of the Roman Catholic Church in 2013, has relaxed the dress code.

The hair and beauty products market is worth billions of pounds.

Many Muslim women cover their hair in public.

FUN
- TIME -

*Whether it is real or artificial,
fake hair is back in fashion.
It's a throwback to ancient hair care!*

Thousands of years ago, the ancient Egyptians wore black or coloured wigs over their shaved heads and were not concerned if they did not look real. Today, the fake wig is back!

PAST FUTURE

Fun wigs do not pretend to look real. They are made from shiny nylon and come in all different colours that are not associated with real hair. They can be pink, blue, bright orange and lurid green. Similar wigs have been popular before, such as for masked balls in sixteenth-century Venice.

Many modern wigs are made in colours that no one could possibly mistake for real hair.

IT'S REAL!

Another twenty-first-century trend that has been around for millennia is wearing other people's hair. Throughout history, women have made wigs from real hair. Roman women cut their slaves' hair to make extensions. Later, in colonial times, Indian and Brazilian women sold their hair to make money. Today, buying real human hair is big business. Fair hair costs three times more than dark hair, because it is in shorter supply. Hair extensions made from real human hair are now so well made that it is almost impossible to tell who is wearing hair extensions and who is not.

A shop displays a range of luxury wigs made from real human hair.

to die for

The Japanese lead the way in wearing fake coloured wigs to copy their favourite characters from films, books, online games and manga comics. The hobby is known as cosplay, an abbreviation of "costume play". Fans have a choice of more than 100 different colours for wigs that range from helmet shapes to Afro styles.

Young Japanese women use wigs as part of their costumes when they dress up as fantasy characters.

TIMELINE

c. 1500 BC	The Assyrians conquer Babylon, introducing their tightly curled hairstyles and beards.
478 BC	Hatshepsut comes to the throne in ancient Egypt. As pharaoh, she wears a false beard.
c. 600 BC	The chignon is a popular hairstyle in Athens in ancient Greece.
146 BC	Rome conquers Greece, and Romans adopt Greek hairstyles.
c. AD 1	The Roman emperor Julius Caesar begins wearing a laurel crown to hide his baldness.
AD 303	The first barber shop opens in Rome.
AD 634	Women start covering their heads in some Muslim countries.
1073	Pope Gregory forbids monks to wear beards. The clean-shaven look soon spreads to men throughout society.
1429	Joan of Arc leads French soldiers into battle against the English at Orléans with her distinctive pageboy haircut.
1558	Queen Elizabeth I comes to the English throne. She begins a fashion for red hair.
1649	Before being beheaded during the English Civil War, King Charles I asks the executioner, "Is my hair well?"
1685	The fontange becomes the most popular hairstyle for women.
c. 1780	Hairstyles up to 90 centimetres (3 feet) tall become popular in France. The hair soon becomes home to vermin.

c. 1785	Beau Brummell becomes leader of the dandies in London. He is said to use three hairdressers at once.
1789	After the French Revolution, the wigs worn by kings and nobles go out of fashion in France.
1798	A tax on wig powder leads to the decline of wigs in Britain.
1804	Josephine becomes empress of France. She leads a reintroduction of hairstyles based on those of ancient Greece.
1837	Victoria becomes queen of Britain. She influences modest, natural styles in which the hair is covered with a bonnet.
1854	British soldiers in the Crimean War grow full beards to help keep their faces warm in winter.
1872	Marcel Grateau invents the Marcel wave, later the basis of the permanent wave (perm).
1905	The African American Sarah Breedlove Davis dreams a recipe for hair cream. Trading as Madam C.J. Walker, she becomes one of the first American woman millionaires.
1918	At the end of World War I, men and women begin to wear their hair short in an echo of military styles during the conflict.
1920s	Young women known as Flappers wear make-up and have their hair cut short.
1950s	The invention of hairspray enables women to pile their hair into "big" styles such as the beehive.
1968	US actress Marsha Hunt causes a sensation on the stage with her "Afro" hairstyle.
1977	Punks appear in Britain and the United States, with coloured, spiked hair.
1984	The word "cosplay" is coined to describe dressing up as fantasy characters, complete with wigs.
2006	Vloggers, sometimes known as beauty YouTubers, begin broadcasting videos about hair and make-up on the internet.

-GLOSSARY-

Afro hairstyle of tight curls sticking out all around the head
auburn reddish-brown colour
bandanas large handkerchiefs worn around the neck or head
Black Pride political movement to celebrate African American culture
bob style in which hair is cut evenly short, above the shoulders
bohemian socially unconventional
bonnet hat tied under the chin with a brim framing the face
bouffant hair styled to stand out from the head in a rounded shape
caustic soda chemical used to make soap and other cleaners
chignon knot or coil of hair at the back of the head
courtiers people at a royal court
dandy man who pays excessive attention to his appearance
Flappers fashionable young women in the 1920s who broke the rules of accepted behaviour and appearance
grunge style of rock music from the 1990s
hair extensions lengths of false hair woven into someone's real hair
immoral having poor standards of behaviour
laurel shrub with dark, glossy leaves
leeches bloodsucking worms used in some medical treatments
macassar oil an oily preparation used to make hair slick and glossy
minerals natural substances such as crystals and salts
modesty quality of not calling attention to oneself
nobility elite, privileged class at the top of society
orthodox following the strict rules of a religion
pageboy cut shoulder-length haircut with the ends curled under
pharaohs rulers of ancient Egypt
platinum silvery-white colour
potash substance made from wood ash
quince pear-shaped Asian fruit
resin sticky substance released from the bark of some trees
Romantic artistic movement based on strong emotions
saffron orange-yellow colouring made from crocus flowers
starch powder made from plants used as a stiffener
symmetrical cut hairstyle in which both sides echo each other exactly
toxic poisonous
vain having excessive pride in one's own appearance
veil piece of fine material worn by women to cover their hair and face
vermin harmful worms or insects

BOOKS

Body Pro: Facts and Figures About Bad Hair Days, Blemishes and Being Healthy (Girlology), Erin Falligant (Raintree, 2019)

A History of Britain in 12 Fashion Items, Paul Rockett (Franklin Watts, 2018)

The Split History of Queen Elizabeth I and Mary, Queen of Scots (Perspectives Flip Books), Nick Hunter (Raintree, 2016)

The Split History of the English Civil War (Perspectives Flip Books), Claire Throp (Raintree, 2016)

WEBSITES

www.dkfindout.com/uk/history/fashion
Find out more about fashion through the ages.

www.bbc.com/bitesize/guides/z3nqsg8/revision/1
Learn more about life in Elizabethan England.

INDEX